'FUNNY, INNOVATIVE, CHEEKY AND ENTERTAINING.'
CENTRE FOR YOUTH LITERATURE

'A ROLLICKING STORY, WITH A HEALTHY DOSE OF HUMOUR AND MAGIC.'
TOHBY RIDDLE

'A TOUR DE FORCE, ENTERTAINING AND FULL OF MOVEMENT.'
THE CHILDREN'S BOOKSELLER, UK

'ROGERS HAS FOUND A MOST DELIGHTFUL WAY TO ENGAGE CHILDREN IN THE ART AND CRAFT
OF STORYTELLING. HIGHLY RECOMMENDED TO KEEP YOUNGER READERS ENGROSSED FOR HOURS.'
★★★★ JUNIOR BOOKSELLER & PUBLISHER

'THE WELL-PACED EVENTS ARE ENTERTAINING, THE SETTING IS ATMOSPHERIC, AND THE
CHARACTERS ARE DRAWN WITH HUMOUR, AFFECTION, AND STYLE.'
THE HORN BOOK, USA

'OBSERVANT READERS OF ALL AGES WILL LOVE EXPLORING THIS ENGAGING FANTASY
AND DEVELOP THEIR OWN MEANINGS THROUGH THE USE OF THEIR IMAGINATION...
A HIGH QUALITY AND BEAUTIFUL PICTURE BOOK.' SAETA NEWSLETTER

'THE BEAUTY OF ROGERS'S BOOKS ARE IN THE MINUTE DETAIL OF HIS ILLUSTRATIONS,
BUT ALSO IN THE FREEDOM HIS PICTURES GIVE YOUNG MINDS TO IMAGINE AND DREAM.'
THE COURIER-MAIL

THE BOY THE BEAR THE BARON THE BARD
Short-listed: Children's Book Council of Australia Awards, Younger Readers
Notable Book: Children's Book Council of Australia Awards, Picture Book
Short-listed: New York Times, Best Illustrated Books of the Year, USA
Short-listed: APA Book Design Awards, Best Designed Children's Picture Book
Short-listed: Aurealis Awards, Children's Book
Notable Book: American Library Association, Children's Book of the Year
Long-listed: Quill Awards, Best Children's Book of the Year, USA
Top 40 Children's Books, *Kirkus Reviews*, USA

MIDSUMMER KNIGHT
Notable Book: Children's Book Council of Australia Awards, Picture Book
Short-listed: Speech Pathology Australia Book of the Year Awards, Lower Primary
Magpies Pick of 2006

THE HERO OF LITTLE STREET
Winner: Children's Book Council of Australia Awards, Picture Book
Honour Book: International Board on Books for Young People
Short-listed: NSW Premier's Literary Awards, Patricia Wrightson Prize for Children's Literature
Short-listed: Aurealis Awards, Children's Illustrated Work/Picture Book
Short-listed: Speech Pathology Australia Book of the Year Awards, Lower Primary
Outstanding International Books, United States Board on Books for Young People, USA

INTRODUCTION

'I was always drawn back to something inside me that had never been fulfilled. The finding of my own unique voice and the telling of stories that were mine and only mine.'

ROGERS, GREGORY (2010)

'Acceptance Speech CBCA Picture Book of the Year Award' *Reading Time* Vol 54, No 4, November, p 5.

———————————————

In 2004, Gregory Rogers published *The Boy the Bear the Baron the Bard*, the first of what was to become a classic series of wordless picture books. Witty, densely suggestive, and action-packed, they contain a mélange of cultural and historical references which demand that the reader pay attention to the sub-text, as much as to plot or theme.

These works draw on Shakespearean drama, traditional folk tales, and on European Renaissance art and music. Gregory's eclectic love for story is obvious, as is his penchant for exploring cultural influences, whether they be contemporary or classical. He enjoyed experimenting in style, loved incorporating references to his particular passions for Renaissance music and culture, but also created a contemporary masterpiece in comic style…a style he'd not employed before in book form, but which he quickly made his own.

When the series was published, Gregory was already an acclaimed artist who had become the first Australian artist to win the prestigious 1994 UK Kate Greenaway Award, presented in 1995 for *Way Home* by Libby Hathorn. His cover art, before and after that, was equally highly regarded. His early picture books explored difficult issues, and were considered ground-breaking in the sense of opening up the form to ideas and images with resonance for both children and young adults.

BBBB, however, was the first book which he had authored alone, followed by his creation of two later books in this series, *Midsummer Knight* (2006) and *The Hero of Little Street* (2009). *BBBB* was listed as one of the *New York Times'* Ten Best Illustrated Picture Books of 2005, and as a Notable Children's Book of the Year by the American Library Association. It received the Australian and NZ Illustration Award 2004 from Illustrators Australia, and was shortlisted in the 2005 Australian Publishers Association Book Design Awards. This, and the two other titles in the trilogy, are also published in the USA by Roaring Brook Press, in Germany by Mauritz Verlag, in France by Dargaud and in The Netherlands by Lemniscaat. *The Hero of Little Street* won the CBCA Picture Book of the Year Award 2010, and was an IBBY Honour List Book in 2011. Prior to his death on 1 May 2013, Gregory had planned to create a fourth and fifth title in the series. Two other picture books were also published posthumously.

Gregory would be so very thrilled to see this volume published, as will be his many future readers.

DR ROBYN SHEAHAN-BRIGHT

Gregory ROGERS

The boy the bear the baron the bard

and other dramatic tales

ALLEN & UNWIN
SYDNEY · MELBOURNE · AUCKLAND · LONDON

FOR ERICA
(FLYING SOLO ISN'T SO SCARY AFTER ALL)

———————————

I HAVE ALWAYS BEEN FASCINATED BY EVERYTHING ELIZABETHAN:
THE CLOTHES, THE MUSIC, THE DANCING, THE FOOD. WHEN I HAD THE
IDEA FOR A STORY ABOUT A YOUNG BOY WHO IS FLUNG THROUGH TIME
TO LAND ON THE STAGE OF THE GLOBE THEATRE IN TUDOR LONDON,
I SAW MY CHANCE TO SHARE THOSE HARSH, DIRTY, BRUTAL, BEAUTIFUL
TIMES WITH OTHERS. I MADE MY WAY THROUGH A MOUNTAIN OF BOOKS
TO DISCOVER ALL THE AMAZING HISTORICAL DETAILS OF THE ERA; THEN
I DRAFTED AND REDRAFTED THE STORY TO MAKE IT RICH AND REAL.

ONE OF THE THINGS I LEARNED WAS THAT SHAKESPEARE'S PLAYS WERE
PERFORMED AT FOUR O'CLOCK ON MIDSUMMER AFTERNOONS. THAT WAS
WHEN I KNEW I HAD THE KEY TO THE MAGIC IN THIS BOOK.

GREGORY ROGERS

The BOY · The BEAR
The BARON · The BARD

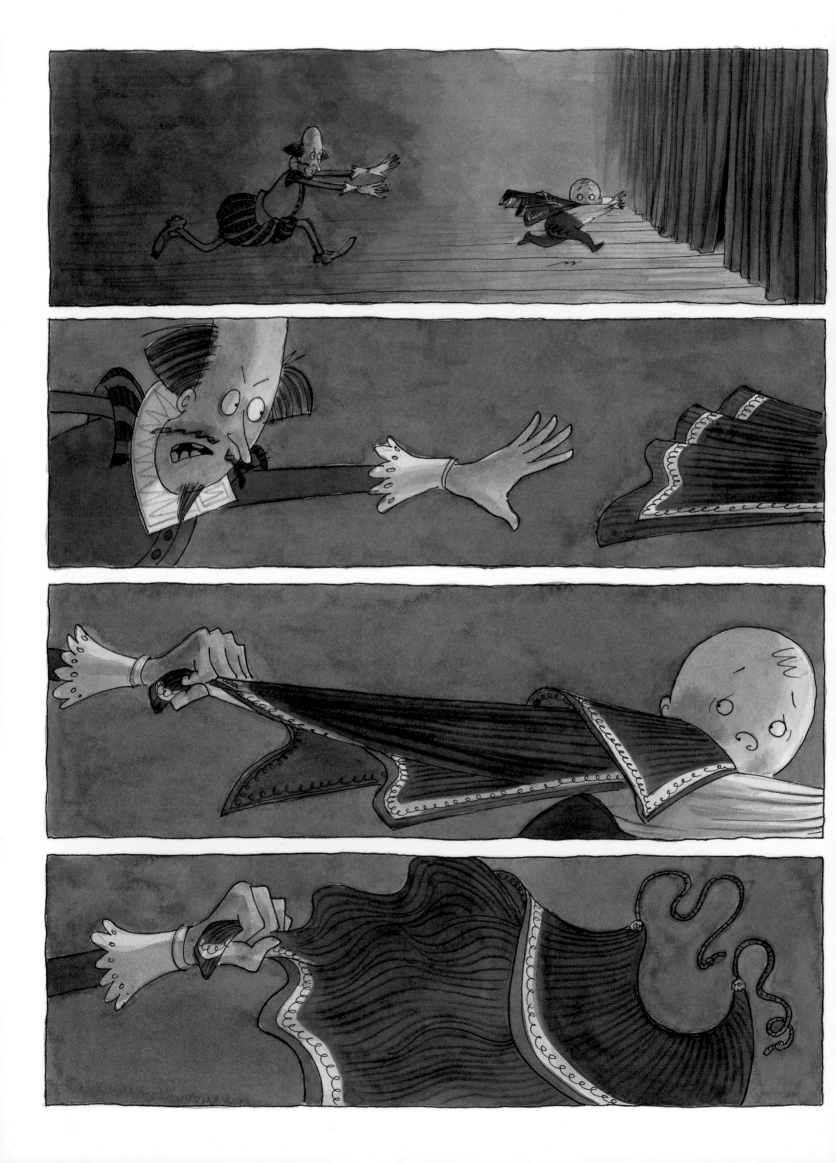

ACKNOWLEDGEMENTS

I WANT TO THANK ALL THOSE PEOPLE WHO HELPED ME TO MAKE THIS BOOK A REALITY. THANKS JENNY THYNNE FOR YOUR HELP WITH ALL THINGS BRITISH, MARGARET CONNOLLY FOR BEING THE BEST AGENT IN THE WORLD AND JODIE WEBSTER FOR YOUR KEEN EYE THAT CAN SPOT A FUMBLE AT FIFTY PACES. THANKS NEAL PORTER FOR SHOWING FAITH IN THE NEW KID ON THE BLOCK. AND THANKS TO MY SUPPORTERS ON THE HOME FRONT, BART, HARRY AND PUDDING.

————————

THE LAST TIME I SAW MY FRIEND THE BEAR HE WAS ADRIFT ON THE THAMES RIVER, ABOUT TO VANISH UNDER THE ARCHES OF OLD LONDON BRIDGE. I CERTAINLY DIDN'T EXPECT TO SEE HIM AGAIN. BUT CHANCE ENCOUNTERS CAN HAVE EXTRAORDINARY OUTCOMES.

I'VE ALWAYS LOVED SHAKESPEARE'S A MIDSUMMER NIGHT'S DREAM. EVER SINCE I SAW AN OLD BLACK AND WHITE MOVIE OF THE PLAY, I HAVE BEEN EXCITED BY THE IDEA OF A MAGICAL FOREST POPULATED WITH MISCHIEVOUS FAERIES. IT WAS IN THAT MYSTERIOUS PLACE THAT I FOUND INSPIRATION AND THE CHANCE TO GIVE THE BEAR A RETURN PERFORMANCE. AND IF YOU LOOK CLOSELY YOU MIGHT EVEN RECOGNISE SOME OF THE OTHER PLAYERS.

GREGORY ROGERS

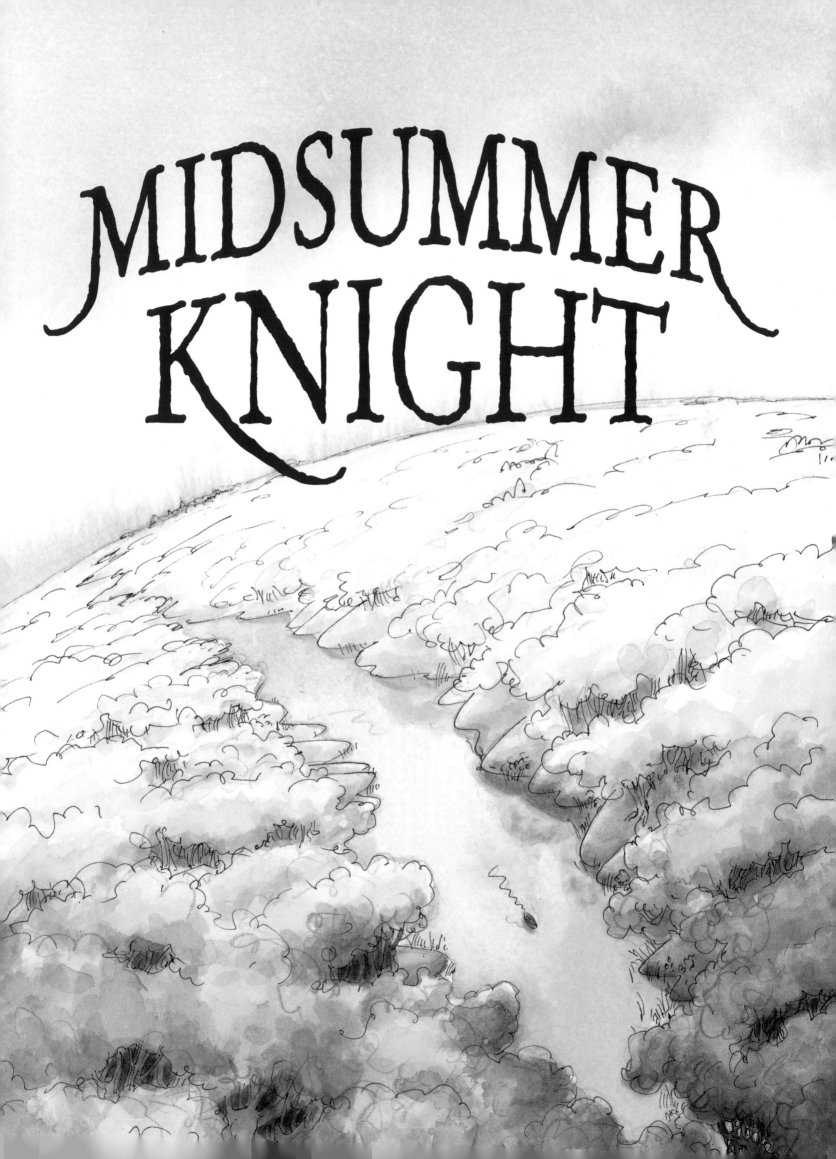

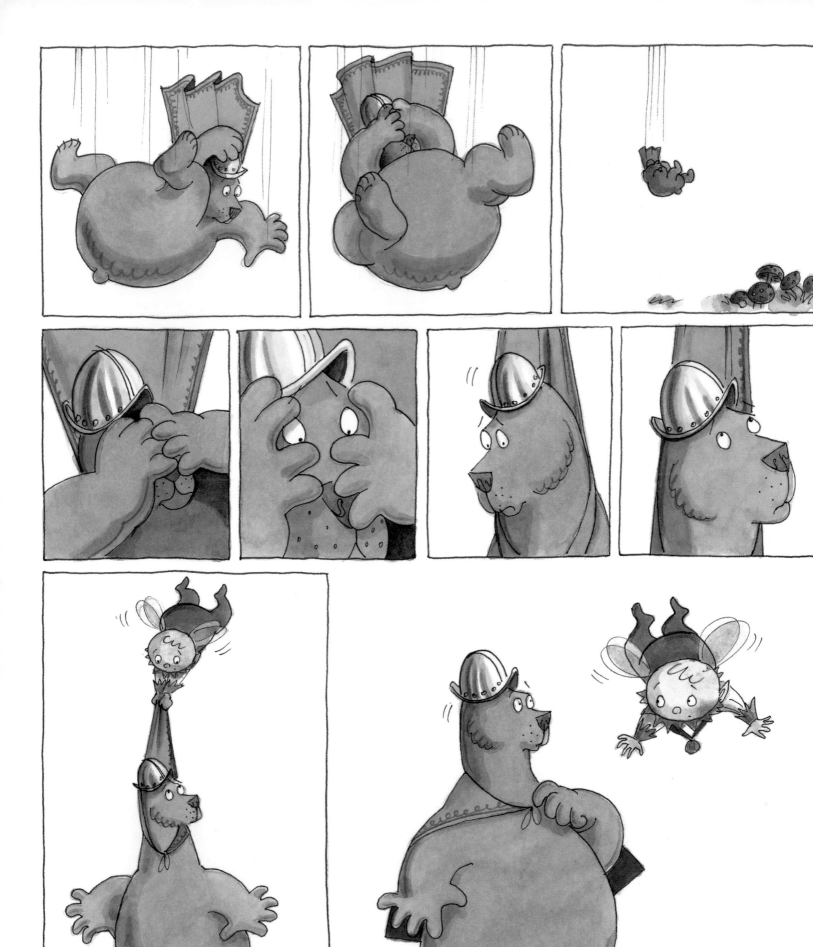

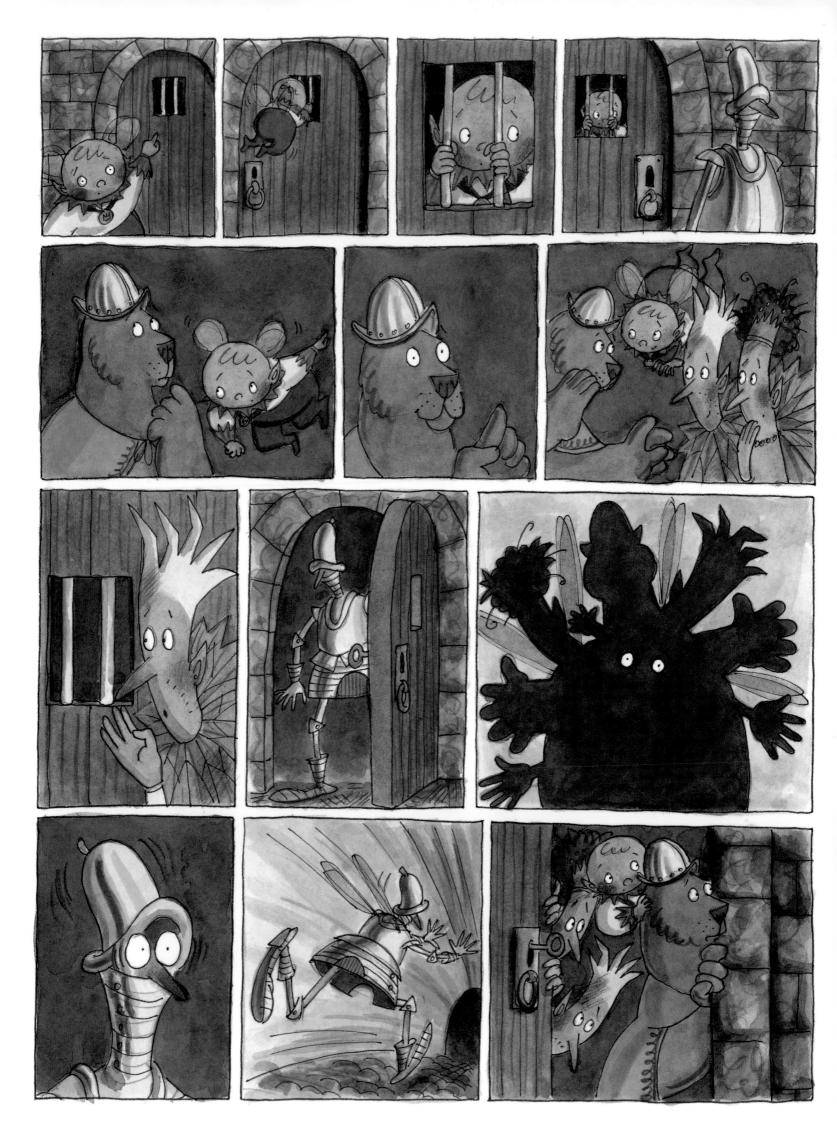

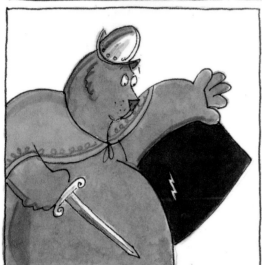

ACKNOWLEDGEMENTS

THANKS TO SIENNA BROWN FOR SHARING HIS JOURNEY WITH ME,
ERICA WAGNER AND JODIE WEBSTER WHO KEPT THE WIND IN MY SAILS,
MARGARET CONNOLLY FOR KEEPING THE WATERS CALM ALONG THE WAY,
NEAL PORTER WHO IS THE BEACON ON FOREIGN SHORES AND BART,
HARRY AND PUDDING FOR KEEPING THE HOME LIGHTS BURNING
FOR WHEN I ARRIVED BACK AT PORT. THANKS TO THE
AUSTRALIA COUNCIL FOR KEEPING THE BOAT AFLOAT.

FOR CATIE CAMPBELL
'FOLLOW YOUR STAR'

———————

As the curtain fell on *The Boy, The Bear, The Baron, The Bard*,
I never quite knew what the Boy would get up to next. I left him
wandering the streets of London. But somehow his irrepressible spirit
has landed him in another amazing predicament. And he discovers
that adventure can be found in the most unlikely of places.

I often wonder about the real lives of people in paintings.
The older the painting, the more curious the people. I have long
admired the paintings of Vermeer and Van Eyck and this book gave
me the perfect opportunity to step inside and see for myself.
Together the Boy and I discovered a mysterious world just beyond
the gilded frame — a world of fun, friendship and fiendish excitement.

GREGORY ROGERS

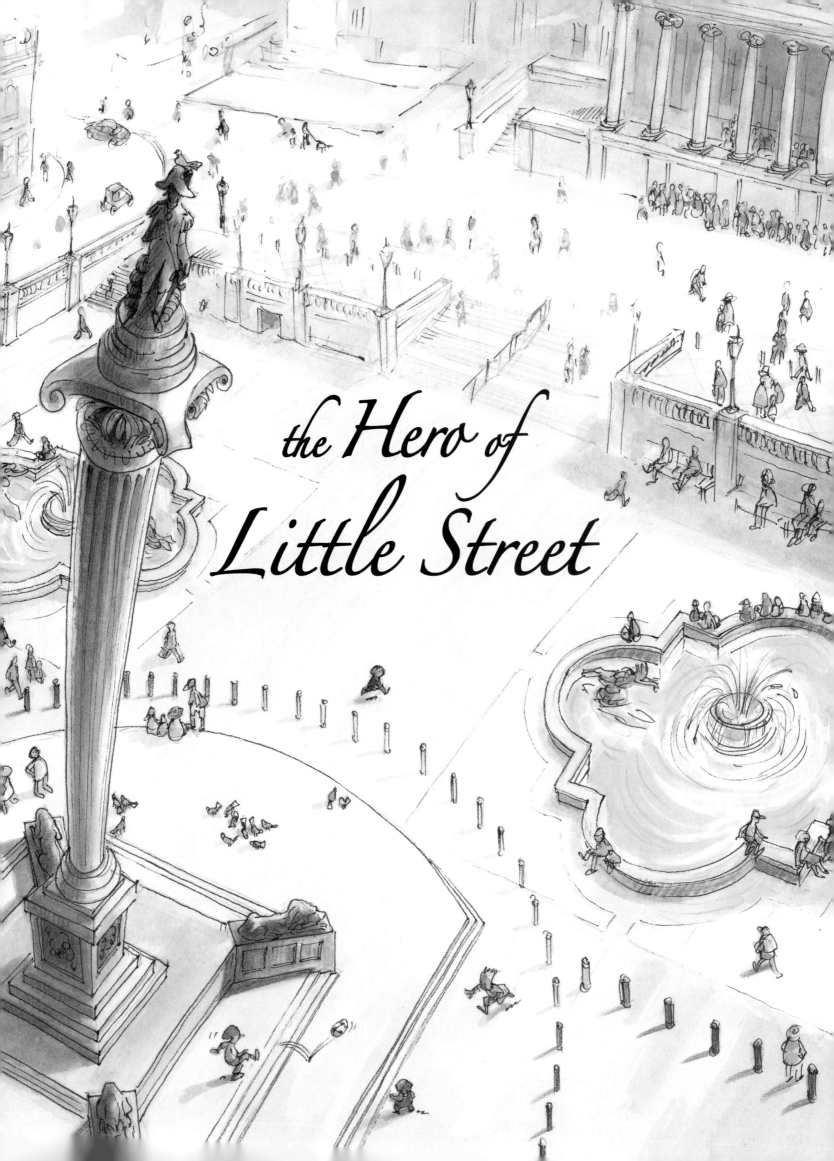

the Hero of
Little Street

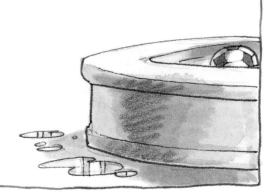

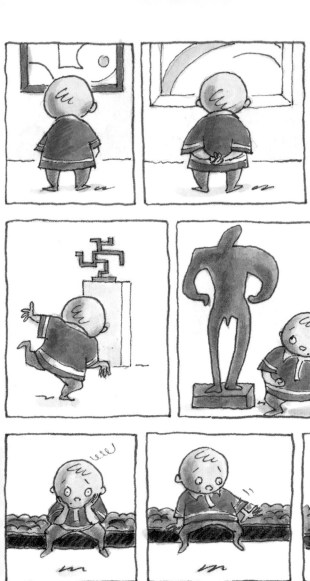

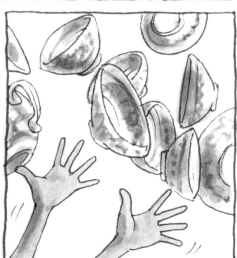

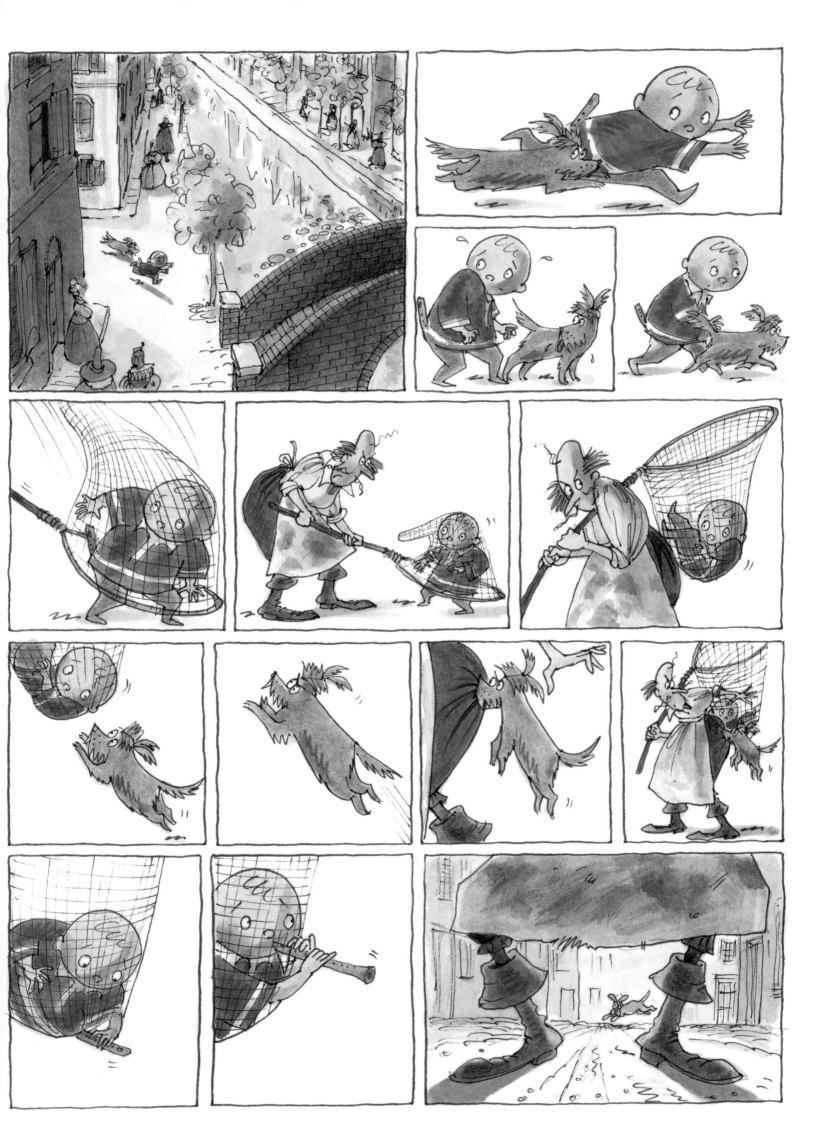

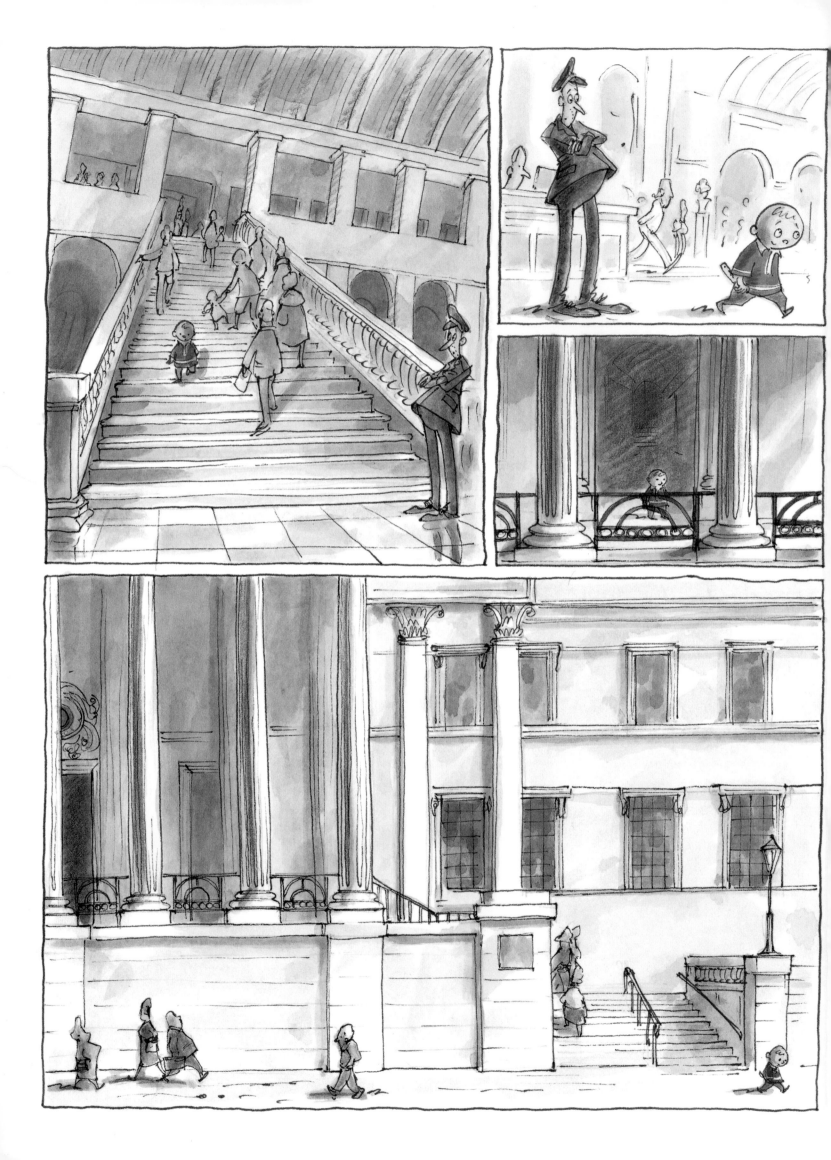

ACKNOWLEDGEMENTS

THANKS TO THE BOY WHO REIGNITED MY LOVE OF JAN VERMEER'S WORLD. AND TO THE ARNOLFINIS, WHOSE DOG ALWAYS LOOKED HAPPIER THAN THEY EVER DID. THANKS TO JODIE WEBSTER AND ERICA WAGNER, MY GUARDIAN ANGELS; MARGARET CONNOLLY, THE VOICE OF REASON AND COMMON SENSE; NEAL PORTER, WHOSE QUIET SMILE MADE THE MEMORY OF ALL THE HARD WORK SEEM TO MELT AWAY; AND TO MY MANY FRIENDS AND FURRY COMPANIONS FOR JUST BEING THERE.

GREGORY ROGERS STUDIED FINE ART AT THE QUEENSLAND COLLEGE OF ART AND WORKED AS A GRAPHIC DESIGNER FOR MANY YEARS BEFORE TAKING UP FREELANCE ILLUSTRATION. HE WAS THE FIRST AUSTRALIAN TO BE AWARDED THE PRESTIGIOUS KATE GREENAWAY MEDAL. BOOK 1 IN THE BOY BEAR SERIES, *THE BOY, THE BEAR, THE BARON, THE BARD*, WAS FIRST PUBLISHED IN AUSTRALIA IN 2004. IT HAS BEEN PUBLISHED IN THE UK, FRANCE, THE NETHERLANDS AND THE USA, AND WAS SHORT-LISTED FOR MANY LOCAL AND INTERNATIONAL AWARDS INCLUDING THE CBCA AWARDS, YOUNGER READERS AND WAS SELECTED AS ONE OF THE TEN BEST ILLUSTRATED PICTURE BOOKS BY THE NEW YORK TIMES IN 2004. BOOK 2 IN THE SERIES, *MIDSUMMER KNIGHT*, WAS A *MAGPIES* PICK OF 2006 AND A CBCA NOTABLE BOOK IN 2007 AND THE FINAL BOOK, *THE HERO OF LITTLE STREET*, WAS THE WINNER OF THE 2010 CHILDREN'S BOOK COUNCIL OF AUSTRALIA PICTURE BOOK OF THE YEAR AWARD. GREG IS MUCH MISSED.